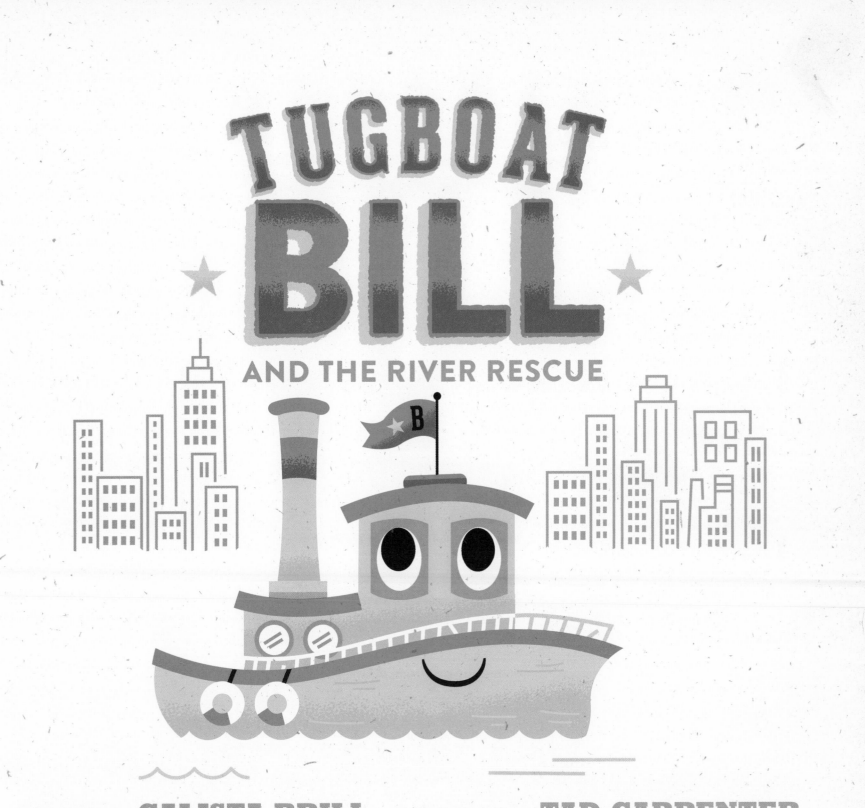

TUGBOAT BILL

AND THE RIVER RESCUE

WRITTEN BY **CALISTA BRILL**   ILLUSTRATED BY **TAD CARPENTER**

HARPER

An Imprint of HarperCollinsPublishers

Tugboat Bill and the River Rescue
Text copyright © 2017 by Calista Brill
Illustrations copyright © 2017 by Tad Carpenter
For information address
HarperCollins Children's Books, a division of HarperCollins Publishers, 195 Broadway,
New York, NY 10007. www.harpercollinschildrens.com
ISBN 978-0-06-236618-4

16 17 18 19 20 SCP 10 9 8 7 6 5 4 3 2 1
❖
First Edition

To Grandpa BILL
and Grandma Romana.
With Love, T.C.

To *my* Grandpa BILL
and to my Gammie.
—C.B.

There is a tugboat, and his name is Bill.

Bill lives on the Hudson River.
The Hudson River is
smooth
	or choppy.
It is blue
	or gray.
It is swift
	or sluggish
depending on the day.

Bill has a captain, Boris.
Boris is
silent
    or humming.
He is sunny
    or sour.
He is sleepy
    or asleep
depending on the hour.

Bill knows a barge, Mabel.
Mabel is
rusty
    and dusty.
She is dented
    and heapy.
She's loyal
    and brave
and just a bit leaky.

Bill and Mabel are friends.

Every day, Bill
booms his engines
wiggles his prow
digs his propellers into the cool, lazy water
and . . .
PUSHES.
(Or pulls.)

Every day, Mabel
squares her shoulders
braces her hull
picks up her huge, heavy load of gravel
and . . .
DOESN'T SINK.
(Hey, you try it sometime.)

The river is home to other ships, too.
They are big
    and graceful.
They are fit
    and prime.
They are haughty
    and vain
almost all of the time.

(They think they are so great.)

The big ships say
that Mabel is
dirty
        squat
listing
        dumpy
awkward
        ugly
silly
        stupid
and (gasp!) boring.

Mabel
squares her shoulders
braces her hull
and pretends she doesn't hear.

But she does.
And so does Bill.

One
busy
  breezy
sparkling
  easy
swiftly
  rushing
river day . . .

SPLASH!

"I'd be scuttled and sunk before
I'd touch THAT thing,"
says one big ship.

"I'd be scuttled and sunk before
I'd let THAT on board,"
says another.

"Of all the nerve,
asking for help,
as if we would ever,
ever,
      EVER
help."

"I didn't need your help anyhow," says the kitten.

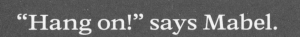

"Hang on!" says Mabel.

"Throw him a rope, Mabel!"
says Bill.
"Climb aboard, kitten,"
says Mabel.

"Zzzz," says Boris.

"Much obliged," says the kitten,
safe and sound.

Bill knows that Mabel is a hero.
And by the next day,
the whole world knows it, too.

The big ships aren't happy.

"I wish *I* had picked up the kitten," says one.

"I wish *I* was a hero like Mabel,"
says a second.

"I wish *I* had a tugboat like Bill,"
says a third big ship.

Bill and Mabel pay them no mind.

They go up and down the
smooth
  choppy
blue
  gray
swift
  and sluggish
Hudson River.

And the kitten goes with them.

And if you go down to the river on a breezy, easy day,
here is what you might see:
a kitten, standing on the prow of
a barge, pushed steady through the water by
a tugboat, whose captain is
                    sound
                              asleep.